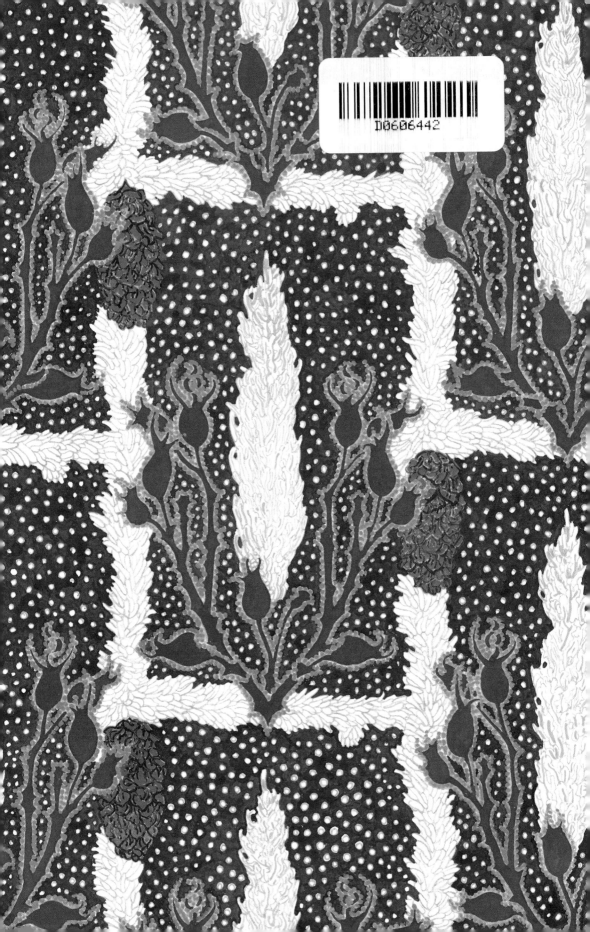

APPLES AND ANGEL LADDERS

A COLLECTION OF PIONEER CHRISTMAS STORIES

WRITTEN BY IRENE MORCK
ILLUSTRATED BY MURIEL WOOD

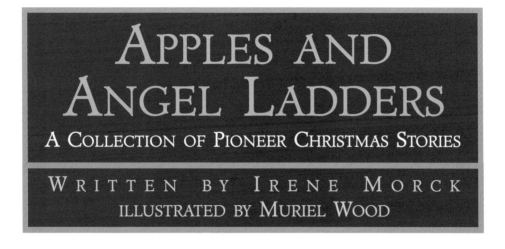

APPLES AND ANGEL LADDERS

A COLLECTION OF PIONEER CHRISTMAS STORIES

WRITTEN BY IRENE MORCK
ILLUSTRATED BY MURIEL WOOD

Fitzhenry & Whiteside

Text copyright © 2001 by Irene Morck
Illustrations copyright © 2001 by Muriel Wood

Published in Canada by Fitzhenry & Whiteside,
195 Allstate Parkway, Markham, Ontario L3R 4T8
Published in the United States by Fitzhenry & Whiteside,
121 Harvard Avenue, Suite 2, Allston, Massachusetts 02134

Printed in Hong Kong

10 9 8 7 6 5 4 3 2 1

National Library of Canada Cataloguing in Publication Data

Morck, Irene
Apples and angel ladders : a collection of pioneer Christmas stories

ISBN 1-55041-6715

1. Christmas stories. 2. Frontier and pioneer life—Prairie Provinces—Fiction. I. Wood,
Muriel II. Title.

PS8576.O628A86 2001   C813'.54   C2001-901079-6
PZ7.M7885Ap 2001

U.S. Cataloging-in-Publication Data
(Library of Congress Standards)

Morck, Irene.
Apples and angel ladders : a collection of pioneer Christmas stories /
written by Irene Morck ; illustrated by Muriel Wood.–1st. ed.
[96] p. : ill. (some col.) ; cm.
Summary: Collection of Christmas stories centering on homesteading life in the West.
IBSN 1-55041-6715
1. Christmas stories, American – Juvenile literature. [1. Christmas stories.] I. Wood,
Muriel, ill. II. Title.
394.2663 [F] 21 2001 AC CIP

Fitzhenry & Whiteside acknowledges with thanks
the Canada Council for the Arts, the Government of Canada through
the Book Publishing Industry Development Program (BPIDP),
and the Ontario Arts Council for their support
of our publishing program.

F
MOR

Design by Wycliffe Smith

This book is for Thora.
It could not have been written without her.
I.M.

For my grandchildren Colin, Lauren and Rachel.
M.W.

This book is a true delight, and children of all ages are in for a treat. The evocative stories in *Apples and Angel Ladders* tell of a time more than eighty years ago, when a Danish family celebrated Christmas in North America. Even though money was scarce, Christmas for the Morck family was a special time of the year. Everyone participated in the holiday preparations. There was much work to be done: finding the perfect tree, making decorations, and baking cookies. The sense of excitement reached its peak when Christmas finally arrived and the festivities were shared with friends.

When I first read this book I wanted to eat an apple, bake peppernodder cookies and make angel ladders (readers will be pleased, as I was, to find instructions for making both angel ladders and peppernodders). But I also thought about my own family's celebrations, and I know you will think of yours. What makes Christmas special for each of us? This collection reminds us to revel in our own past. We can all discover our history by asking our parents, grandparents, aunts and uncles to tell their own stories. Those childhood memories and customs from around the corner or across the globe will make the holiday a time to cherish. We all have exciting stories hidden in our own past.

Apples and Angel Ladders, with beautiful illustrations by Muriel Wood, allows us to share in the fun, excitement and sometimes sadness of one family's past Christmases. This book also encourages us to discover and honor our own unique family traditions and stories for all the Christmases to come.

KEN SETTERINGTON

INTRODUCTION

Did your family—your great-grandparents, grandparents, or maybe even your parents—come from another country? Does your family still observe special cultural or religious traditions that were carried from their homeland? If so, those traditions are probably wrapped in stories that show the struggle and inner strength of people who made their way in a new and sometimes harsh land. That's what happened in my family. My father, Archie Morck, was the son of Danish immigrants, and our Christmas celebrations were filled with stories.

No matter how well immigrants adapt to life in a new country, they still treasure the traditions of their native homes. For many pioneer settlers in North America, Christmas was a time to honour their heritage, both spiritual and cultural. During those long and often bleak winters, Christmas brought families and their communities together. The festivities gave pioneers a chance, for even a little while, to forget their hardships and concentrate on beauty and meaning. Talk to the people who lived in those days, and you'll often see their eyes glow as they recount Christmas stories.

My father loved to tell family anecdotes, especially those from his pioneer childhood, including experiences of Christmas past. At the age of sixty-four my father was seriously injured in a car accident, then had a stroke and a heart attack. When it was obvious that he couldn't work any more, I asked, "Now, Dad, would you please tape or write down some things about your life?"

Fortunately my father complied. In his stroke-slurred voice he made twelve hours of tapes. With shaky hands he scrawled 800 pages. In those tapes and in those hand-written notes he told of the pioneer days, the Depression, his struggle to finish his schooling, his life as a parent of seven rambunctious children (one of them was me, of course) and his experiences as a Lutheran pastor in various parts of Canada.

When my father died at the age of sixty-six, I assumed that I'd learn nothing else about his childhood, but his sister Esther told me a few more incidents. After Esther died, I heard many additional stories from my dad's sister Thora. Thora has contributed in another way too—helping me recount the family's history as accurately as possible by patiently answering my endless questions.

I used the first one-third of my father's memoirs—the adventures of his pioneer childhood and the Depression years—for the book *Five Pennies: A Prairie Boy's Story*, published in 1999.

Although *Five Pennies* was originally written for an adult audience, I've been thrilled to see how well it has been received by children of all ages. To my delight, many teachers have used my father's stories in their social studies classes, even in elementary schools. This Christmas collection, on the other hand, was written especially for children. But I hope that adults of all ages will find much to enjoy in its pages as well.

With the exception of one brand new story, the adventures in this Christmas collection have all been adapted and expanded from *Five Pennies*. These stories are from my dad's childhood years in the Danish pioneer community of Dickson, located in Alberta's central woodlands. Today, there are still plenty of artifacts from Dickson's early days. Carl Christiansen's General Store is now a museum, which was officially opened by the Queen of Denmark in 1991. In the museum are several items that belonged to the Morck family.

The Morck's log home is long gone, but their two-storey lumber house (built in 1931) is still in use, and the original homestead land is still farmed by grandchildren of 'Mama' and 'Papa' Morck.

"Are all those stories really true?" I'm asked over and over again. Yes, these things really did happen. Yes, all these characters certainly lived. Of course it isn't always possible for memories to retrieve every detail, nor for memories to agree always on the details they do produce. But I can say in all honesty that they are as true as hearts and memories can make them.

And, no, I'm not the same Irene as the Irene in these stories. But, yes, I am named after her—my father's little sister.

Christmas is Coming

1919

"Archie, hold your little sister." Mama handed me the wailing six-month-old baby. "Let me add the last bits of flour. We have to get the texture just right for the dough to roll out."

It was early December. We were making pebbernodders for Christmas. Christmas was the only time we ever had these tiny, spicy Danish cookies. I was nine years old and my brother Arnfeld was almost seven. Making pebbernodders was one of our favourite jobs.

While Mama had cuddled Irene and given directions, I had made the pebbernodder dough all by myself. I beat the eggs. I mixed the sugar with butter and lemon juice. I sifted in the flour, spices and baking powder. Now I held the crying baby as Mama added more flour, in tiny amounts, testing the dough each time. "You can always add flour," she said. "But it's hard to subtract flour." I laughed.

My baby sister Irene kept crying no matter how I rocked her in my arms, even when I cooed to her. Irene cried much of the time, day and night, as though tormented by dreadful pain.

Finally Mama had the texture of the dough exactly right. "That's it," she said. "Now you boys roll the dough into snakes." She took the crying baby from me, smiled at her tenderly and said, "How are you doing, my little one?"

Using the palms of our hands, Arnfeld and I began rolling the dough into long, thin snake shapes. "Me too," said our almost three-year-old sister Esther. "I make snakes."

"You're too young," said Arnfeld.

Esther howled, adding to the noise of Irene's crying that already filled our two-room log house. "Esther can roll snakes too," said Mama. Esther immediately quit crying and made a face at Arnfeld.

"Careful, Esther," said Mama, "your face might freeze ugly, just like that. Archie, you start chopping up the snakes."

As Arnfeld and Esther rolled the dough, I used a sharp knife, cutting across the long snakes, to make hundreds of tiny cookies about the size and shape of a fingertip. Arnfeld and I spread the miniature cookies on Mama's metal cookie sheets.

Mama gently laid her squalling baby in the cradle. It was time to bake the pebbernodders.

"Hi there," I said to Irene, as I rocked her cradle. "Someday we'll let you make pebbernodders." She sobbed a bit softer, moving her eyes in response to the sound of my voice.

Everybody said that Irene was the prettiest baby. She had soft, blond hair and a beautiful face. Her arms and legs looked the same as those of any other baby. Her wide, grey-blue eyes moved towards sounds, but her eyes never followed the motion of anything silent. She'd been born blind. Our whole family had almost died from the Spanish flu in February. Mama had been pregnant with Irene then. Unlike many Spanish flu victims, we'd all survived, but Mama's new baby had taken the damage.

While Irene cried, Mama baked the pebbernodders. I breathed in the spicy fragrance coming from the cookies in the oven of the wood-burning stove. When the pebbernodders were baked golden brown, Mama slid them onto the paper-covered table so Arnfeld, Esther and I could load the cookie sheets again and again. We'd be using these cookies not only for serving throughout the Christmas season, but also for playing a special Christmas game.

Papa came in for coffee. He'd been putting in long days, using a handsaw to cut down dozens of tall trees for next year's firewood. He had to chop off the branches with an ax, and haul loads of the tree-length logs home on the bobsled with our big,

strong team of horses. He could make three or four trips a day. This was his third trip since the morning.

"You must have smelled pebbernodders a half a mile out there in the field," said Mama. "You timed it just right."

"Papa," said Esther, "I can make snakes. For pebbernodders."

"It's good you can do something more than just cause trouble." Papa slurped his hot coffee and gulped down a couple of handfuls of the tiny pebbernodder cookies before he ate a piece of brown bread with cheese. He turned to Mama. "If you and Archie milk the cows tonight, I think I have time to bring in one more load before it gets dark."

Mama nodded. "Just a few more days of logging and you might have enough wood. There's a mighty big pile of logs already."

Papa said, "We're going to need a mountain of firewood this coming year for heating and cooking and for boiling water to wash all the diapers." Mama looked down, silent, her smile fading. She was pregnant with her fifth child. Mama already looked so tired from lack of sleep and worry over Irene.

"I'd better get going," said Papa, "or it will be dark before I even make it out to the woods."

Irene was wailing again. I picked her up and held her. She flopped against my arms. Irene seemed so weak for a six-month-old. Would she ever be able to lift her head right off a pillow or hold herself in a sitting position as other babies her age did so easily? I knew we were all wondering such things. But Irene kept trying, trying so hard, moving her head and arms and legs.

After Papa left, I helped Mama wash the utensils. Arnfeld and Esther took out the T. Eaton catalogue to play a game— choosing one Christmas present from every single page. They found it hilarious when they had to choose from a page of only women's nightgowns, or a page of shovels, or one with only paintbrushes and paint cans, or a page of only men's boots. Arnfeld rocked Irene in her cradle while they played. Our baby sister seemed to settle down a bit as Arnfeld and Esther giggled at their silly choices.

We loved playing with the T. Eaton catalogue. What a thrill it was each time a new one arrived. Everyone in our community jokingly referred to the T. Eaton catalogue as "the Farmer's Bible." For people living in remote areas, the catalogue was an armchair trip to any store in any city. If you had the money, you could buy anything from the catalogue—horse harness, wagons and carriages, clothes, jewellery, farm machinery, even complete materials with instructions to build a house. And, of course, dolls, games and toys.

The best part was that we'd each be getting at least one Christmas present from the catalogue. That gave us a thrill when we looked through its pages. Some years we might even get more than one present from the catalogue.

Every summer Mama raised some extra chickens to sell in the fall, to help make money for groceries, clothes, and other essential things. With some of the money from these chickens, Mama always financed our Christmas presents.

This year quite a bit of Mama's chicken money had been used for an appointment with a doctor. Almost no one in our community ever went to a doctor, not even for a baby's birth. But Mama and Papa were so desperate about Irene that they'd taken her to the closest doctor, to Innisfail, twenty-five miles away over rutty roads. With the team and wagon, the trip had taken about seven hours each way. All the doctor had said was, "There's nothing I can do for her. She'll probably grow out of it."

When we finished washing the baking utensils, Mama and I packed the freshly made pebbernodders carefully into tins. After supper, as usual, Mama scrubbed our school clothes. She rubbed them against the glass ridges of the washboard and dipped them into the sudsy water of her metal wash pan. We children rocked our crying baby sister and played with the catalogue, trying to guess our presents. "Esther, I bet you get that stuffed bear," Arnfeld said. "Or maybe that doll." He had pointed to a fabulous doll.

Esther beamed. "No, *that* one!" We laughed. She was pointing to a smaller, much less expensive doll. Papa looked up from his reading and said, "Esther's smart for her age."

"Arnfeld," I said, "I bet you're going to get that game of checkers."

"Naw," he said, "it will be that board game. Because Mama likes to play board games…when she has time." Mama grinned and kept scrubbing.

We knew our presents wouldn't be expensive, but that didn't matter one bit to us. Mama was the one who sent in the catalogue order. She seemed to be able to pick perfect presents to have under the tree for each of us on Christmas Eve.

To a Dane—even in our Danish pioneer community of Dickson in the woodlands of central Alberta—Christmas meant Christmas Eve. The night of December twenty-fourth was when Danes had their big meal and opened their presents. Christmas day was simply for going to church and for visiting.

For weeks, Mama, Arnfeld and I (with Esther trying to help) had used any spare time to get ready for Christmas Eve. We spent hours making decorations to cover the beautiful spruce tree that Papa would cut and put up in our home on the morning of the twenty-fourth.

The day after we made pebbernodders, Mama took time to help us with our decorations. "I'm going to make a Christmas rose," said Arnfeld. By himself he folded a long strip of red crepe paper, doubling it again and again until it was less than two inches wide. Mama helped him with the scissors to cut into the thick fold on each side, slicing about two-thirds of the way down.

Arnfeld unfolded the strip. Then, with a bit of help from Mama, he used a knitting needle to roll the edges of each pair of slits toward each other to make connected petals. Taking a deep breath, he pleated the strip as evenly as he could, around and around itself to make the layers of a flower, bunching the paper at the bottom so the petals flared out. Mama helped Arnfeld wrap a piece of thin wire around the bottom to hold it all together.

"That's a nice flower," said Mama.

Esther decided she wanted to make a flower too. She wouldn't let Mama help her much, so of course Esther's flower ended up looking mighty ragged. But Mama smiled. "It's a flower that's been out in the wind, that's all."

"I'm going to make an angel ladder," I said. I cut a long, narrow strip of soft pink tissue paper, folded the strip in half the long way first, then folded the other way, doubling it over and over. As evenly as possible, I snipped a row of slits along the folded edge, cutting almost to the outside edge.

"Remember to cut into the folds at the ends too," Mama said, "or your ladder will be missing some rungs."

When I tried to open the soft paper, the slits caught on each other and tore a bit, but Mama helped me open it more carefully. It delighted me to see the tiny angel ladder rungs that would reach up and down between the Christmas tree's branches.

Irene was crying pretty hard by then. I picked her up and talked to her so Mama, Arnfeld and Esther could keep making decorations. Arnfeld was working now on a heart-shaped basket. His hands clumsy, he cut out two pieces of glossy paper— one red and one blue—then cut their ends into strips. He began to weave the strips together into the heart shape, but got mixed up on the weaving pattern, and the basket couldn't open. He made a face when I laughed.

Arnfeld started again. This time, with Mama's guidance, he made a good basket. Mama held his basket while Arnfeld glued a strip of paper across the opening for a handle to hang on a tree branch.

To me, the whole Christmas season was the best time of the year. I loved our family preparations, our Christmas celebrations and gifts. Besides, there were all the community preparations for the church's Christmas concert, and the concert itself on the night of December twenty-sixth.

One evening, about a week before Christmas, our whole

family rode in the bobsled to Dickson. This was the night the community gathered in the church basement to make decorations for the big Christmas tree at the church. Irene seemed to like the motion of the bobsled and the sound of the horses' harness jingling. She quit crying for most of the four-mile trip.

From the moment we arrived, other women took turns holding and comforting Irene. I loved how Mama's eyes lit up as she chatted and laughed with everyone. Papa looked so happy and relaxed too.

Gas lamps hung from the ceiling, hissing overhead. All of the adults—men and women—sat at a long table making decorations. They made fancy flowers, some of crepe paper, some of tissue paper. They made flawless palm-sized, heart-shaped candy baskets, each basket woven from two different colours of thick, glazed paper. Even the farmers with their thick, calloused hands created dainty, perfectly symmetrical angel ladders from tissue paper.

Older children who proved themselves careful enough were allowed to help. I made a couple of paper flowers, but they were messy compared to the adults' creations, so I ran off to play with the other kids.

No one seemed to mind that my baby sister was still crying. In fact, some of my friends took turns holding her, chattering away to her. Once in a while Irene would quit crying, and whoever happened to be holding her at the time felt victorious.

We kids had plenty of fun playing that night, but I thought the adults were having even more fun—telling stories and jokes, chatting, laughing—as their busy fingers worked to create splendid decorations. You could almost taste the excitement.

At long last the adults finished their cutting, weaving and gluing. We little ones looked on, salivating, while they filled the woven heart-shaped paper baskets with a few (mostly store-bought!) candies. Children were never allowed to help with this task, nor were any of us ever allowed to snitch samples.

Then came the most exciting task to watch—the filling of the brown paper bags. There'd be one tiny brown paper bag for each person. The adults stuffed the bags with candies of many colours: hard candies, some striped, some in ribbon shapes, some peppermints, plus a few peanuts, and—most wondrous of all—an apple. A real apple, the only apple we'd get all year.

Fresh fruit was expensive. Most families, including ours, could not afford to buy any fresh fruit. We enjoyed berries, which cost nothing and were plentiful for picking in the area. But we cherished two special treats in the year—this apple at Christmas, and one orange given to each of us at the Dominion Day picnic on July First.

Surely nothing in the world could be more wonderful than Christmas, I thought. Breathing deeply the sweet smell of apples, I watched as the fancy decorations, candy-filled paper baskets and bulging brown paper bags were all packed carefully into boxes.

To finish off the exciting evening, the choir had its final carol practice. Listening to the magnificent Christmas carols excited me even more. Irene seemed to love the music too. Her crying eased, and she drifted off to sleep for a few minutes.

Music swelled through the church basement, amidst the aroma of coffee brewing on the wood-burning stove and Danish pastry heating in the oven. Before we went home, we all had '*kaffe*'. Whenever and wherever Danes gathered for social occasions, coffee, sandwiches, cookies and Danish pastry would be served. But Danes referred to all of this simply as ''. We went home in a great mood.

A few days later, just before Christmas, we all gathered back in Dickson to decorate the Christmas tree at the church. One of the men of the congregation had cut the tree—a fabulous spruce, taller than any person. Living in a woodlands area, we knew it wasn't hard to find great spruce trees, but whoever cut the Christmas tree for the church always tried his best to find one that was superb.

This year's tree was at least ten feet high. It was fragrant, bushy, perfectly-shaped, with balanced, tapered branches and millions of thick, silky, dark needles. "I really do think this one is the best, most beautiful Christmas tree we've ever had," people said. But they said that every year.

Only the adults decorated the Christmas tree. They stretched angel ladders up and down from branch to branch. They hung candy-laden paper baskets from the boughs. They attached spring-clip holders at the end of the spruce branches and put a small, slender candle into each holder. Irene cried through most of that evening too, but as always, people took turns holding her so Mama got to help with the joyful task of decorating.

At last the tallest man in our community stood tip-toe on a stool, arms stretched high, to crown the tree with the shining star made of gold and silver paper. Everyone gasped in admiration and excitement, then said again that this, surely, was the most beautiful tree we'd ever had for the church.

Again, " was served. Smelling the spruce needles, listening to the happy voices, watching the tree and its decorations, I wondered how I could possibly wait.

Tomorrow was Christmas Eve.

CHRISTMAS, AFTER ALL

1 9 2 2

IN SEPTEMBER, SEVERAL CHICKEN-HUNGRY COYOTES HAD BEEN TRYING to sneak into our yard, even when we were home. One Sunday afternoon, as our family was climbing into the wagon to visit the neighbours, Mama said, "Maybe we should shut the chickens into the chicken house."

Papa frowned. "Why didn't you think of doing this sooner?"

"Sometimes it's hard to think of everything, you know," said Mama, easing herself onto the front seat of the wagon, our one-week-old baby sister Alice in her arms. "Archie, run and lure the chickens in with some grain. Quick."

My nine-year-old brother Arnfeld jumped down to help me. Our little sisters Esther and Thora began to climb down from the wagon too, but Papa growled, "You two stay here. It'll take a day to load the whole family up again."

Papa held the horses' reins, sighing impatiently. "Hurry, Archie." Arnfeld and I ran to get a pail of grain to lure the cackling chickens into their little wooden house. Then I closed the small door at the bottom so they couldn't escape.

We left the yard with our chickens safely locked in their crowded wooden coop on that beautiful sunny day even though they would have been much happier outside, wandering our homestead farmyard and feeding on bugs and grass.

After a pleasant visit with the neighbours, we headed back to our farm, still chatting and laughing.

The first thing we noticed as we drove past the chicken coop was the silence. Normally any chickens, especially when they're cooped up, make plenty of noise.

Then we saw a few bloody feathers scattered around on the ground.

Papa yanked the horses to a stop.

I raced to the chicken coop and flung the door open. Dead, all of them. Our chickens were dead, scattered about in blood and churned-up dirt. The chicken house sat right on the ground, with no floor. Beside one wall I saw a hole in the dirt— a tunnel—much too small for coyotes to have made. "Skunks," I said in disgust. "They dug in and killed the chickens." I sniffed the faint smell of skunk. "They killed them all."

The rest of the family were standing beside me now, their eyes wide in horror. "How come there isn't much skunk smell?" asked Arnfeld.

"They spray only when they're upset," muttered Papa. "These skunks were feasting on chickens. Why should they be upset?" He turned to Mama, glaring. "Some idea we had to trap the chickens so a family of skunks could tunnel in and help themselves. Now there won't be one extra penny for anything this year. There won't be any Christmas presents, that's for sure. Not one single present."

Arnfeld, Esther and Thora began to cry. No Christmas presents. I stood silent and numb, looking at the poor, dead creatures.

So this year, just because of the skunks, there'd be no presents for our family on Christmas Eve.

As Christmas Eve approached, closer and closer, I wondered how it would be to have no presents, not even one. Maybe I could think of something to make for each member of my family so that no one would be too saddened by getting nothing. There was Mama, Papa, Arnfeld, five-year-old Esther, two-year-old Thora, and our baby sister Alice. Just thinking of the list made me feel helpless. What could a kid make anyway? And for so many people! I thought and thought about it, but hadn't had any luck yet with ideas for presents.

Someone was missing from the list of our family members. My little sister Irene. It was already more than two years since she had died. Why did it still hurt so much to even think of her? This Christmas my sister Irene would have been three-and-a-half, old enough to yearn for Christmas presents.

All through December, Arnfeld, Esther, Thora and I spent hours making Christmas decorations. This year there wasn't money for crepe paper to make flowers, but we threaded spruce cones into garlands for the Christmas tree. This year there was no money for tissue paper to create angel ladders, nor money for glossy paper to weave little heart-shaped baskets. But we cut up pages from old T. Eaton catalogues to make our paper ladders and baskets.

Even though we knew we weren't going to get anything, we spent many hours poring through the catalogue, taking turns to choose on each page what would have been our favourite present.

We used what sugar could be spared to create homemade candies. And we still baked thousands of tiny pebbernodder cookies, which filled the house with their fragrance.

More days went by, and still I hadn't thought of any presents that I could make. Our tree should have at least some packages under it for Christmas Eve, when we always opened our presents. Might as well just give up, I finally told myself. Nobody was expecting anything this year anyway.

There wouldn't even be money for Mama to buy wool to knit any of us a pair of socks or mitts for Christmas. There wouldn't be wool for even a pair of booties for our baby sister Alice.

Mama didn't have a spinning machine, so she couldn't spin our own sheep's wool into yarn for knitting. She just washed and carded the wool, then traded it at Carl Christensen's general store for wool yarn. This year our wool had all been traded to buy shoes, overalls, cloth, sugar, salt and other necessities.

On December twenty-fourth, as always, Papa cut a beautiful spruce tree for our home. We had so much fun decorating it that afternoon, I almost forgot about Christmas presents.

When the early winter darkness crept in, we lit the kerosene lamps, which threw soft patches of yellow light throughout the two rooms of our log house. The delicious, pungent smell of Danish red cabbage, cooking in its vinegar-and-sugar sauce, tickled our noses. From the oven came the fabulous aroma of our best cut of roast pork.

There was a knock on the door. That would be Carl Lorenzen and Marius Thomsen, two of the community's bachelors invited to join our Christmas Eve celebrations. I ran to open the door. Our visitors stamped the snow off their boots and came in, their cheeks rosy, their eyes shining.

After the festive Christmas Eve meal, Papa and the two men moved into the sitting room (which also served as the bedroom) to visit. Mama, helped by Arnfeld and me, rushed through the dishes and the kitchen clean-up. Esther dried the silverware. Thora tugged at Mama's apron and chattered.

At last we were together in the sitting room, around the spruce tree. Our homemade decorations looked just fine. Papa read the Christmas story from Luke, Chapter Two, and prayed—a long prayer that left Arnfeld, Esther, me, and especially little Thora, squirming restlessly. Baby Alice slept blissfully in her cradle.

Finally it was time for Mama to light the candles on the tree. We turned down the kerosene lamps, our hearts pounding with excitement as each candle glowed to life.

Joining hands, we formed a circle and strode around and around the tree, lustily singing—off-key—every word of our beloved Danish Christmas carols, breathing deeply the smell of candle wax and spruce, as the candlelight sparkled in our eyes. Our tall shadows danced on the walls and ceiling.

When we ran out of carols, we blew out the candles to save them for New Year's Eve, and turned up the kerosene lamps. This was the time we normally distributed the gifts. Of course, this year, the space under the Christmas tree was empty.

To my amazement, Mama reached behind the couch and put four small packages under the tree. The packages were wrapped in used tissue paper. Mama let the unexpected presents sit under the tree for a few minutes while we all murmured in wonder. Then she reached down and handed one to each of us— Arnfeld, Esther, Thora, and me.

Trying not to tear the paper in our excitement, we opened our gifts. There was a pair of knitted mitts for each of us, all four pairs of mitts made from the same dark-green wool. Laughing, Mama fitted a tiny pair of dark-green booties onto Alice's wiggling feet.

Where did Mama get that wool? It looked familiar. Then it hit me. Mama had unravelled one of her own two sweaters to make new mitts for us.

Even in a normal year the chickens didn't bring much money, so our Christmas presents had always been frugal. But to us they had always seemed special. Besides a new shirt or coat, hand-knit socks or mittens, there usually had been at least one toy or game for each of us from the T. Eaton catalogue, and usually a twenty-five-cent doll for Esther.

This Christmas Eve, Arnfeld and I raved over our new mitts.

Mama looked grateful. Thora, too young to remember last year's Christmas presents, was also content with her new mittens. But I could see that Esther remembered well the games and dolls from Christmas Eves past. Esther looked sad, and so did Mama whenever she glanced at my sister's dismal face.

In desperation, I went out to my lean-to bedroom, to the drawer under my bed where I kept my clothes and possessions. I took out the picture from the old calendar that Mama had given me two whole years before, when 1920 ended. She'd given it to me because I loved it so much—that brightly-coloured calendar picture of a little boy and girl with their beautiful pet collie.

I'd never hung the picture on my wall because I didn't want the colour to get faded, the paper tattered, or the surface marred with fly specks. Instead, I'd kept that calendar picture stored carefully. I'd look at it almost every day, then gently place it back into the bottom of my drawer. Now I took the picture out, gave it one long, loving gaze, hid it under my shirt and headed for the kitchen.

Out in the kitchen I found a piece of brown paper that had been used to wrap some sugar we'd bought at the general store. Carefully I rolled the pretty calendar picture, wrapped the brown paper around it, and tied the tube with a string.

Back into the living room I went. "Here, Esther," I said, handing it to my little sister. "It's another Christmas present for you."

She looked puzzled, almost suspicious. But when she opened it, her eyes lit up. She hugged the picture to her chest.

The best part of all was the smiles I got from Mama, our two guests and, yes, even from Papa too. I felt on top of the world.

After opening our presents, we always spent the rest of Christmas Eve playing games. It didn't matter that we had no new games to play this year. Our favourite Christmas game, anyway, was played with the spicy little pebbernodder cookies.

The adults visited while we children played with the pebbernodders, hiding the tiny cookies in our clenched hands, letting the other kids guess how many we had hidden, passing the handful each time onto the victor, eating the cookies as we

played with them. So what if the pebbernodders looked a bit grubby after being hidden in our sweaty palms? We ate the miniature cookies until our stomachs could hold no more.

Eventually it was time for Arnfeld and me to say our groggy goodnights. By then it was hours past our usual bedtime.

Esther had already gone to bed long before, happily clutching her new mitts and her pretty calendar picture.

Had there ever been a better Christmas Eve?

THE CHRISTMAS CONCERT

1 9 2 3

CHRISTMAS DAY. ONLY ONE MORE NIGHT UNTIL THE CONCERT.

Esther, Arnfeld, Thora and I yawned a lot on the morning of Christmas Day. We'd gone to bed late the night before, after opening our presents and playing with our new toys and games.

No matter how tired we might be from our family festivities, we still had to get to Dickson by eleven o'clock that morning for the church service. Everyone in the community was there on Christmas Day—even those few people who hadn't attended church since Easter.

Our team of horses—Jack and Old Sock—pulled us in the bobsled the four miles to Dickson. Papa drove the horses. Mama, pregnant, sat beside him on the front seat of the grain box, holding our one-year-old sister Alice. Arnfeld, Esther, Thora, and I perched on board benches in the back. We cuddled under blankets, our hands warm in the green woollen mittens that Mama had knit for us the Christmas before.

The "grain box" was long, narrow and deep, made of rough lumber. In the winter a grain box sat on runners—the outfit was called a bobsled. In summers we lifted the grain box onto a set of wooden wagon wheels and called the rig a lumber wagon (or just "wagon"). Pioneer farmers used a grain box to haul anything from hay to hogs, from grain to grandmothers. There was no suspension or springs of any kind under a grain box, winter or summer. Today, we bumped and swayed over the wind-swept snowdrifts.

All the way to church that morning in the grain box, I thought of the Christmas concert. I had two resolutions.

For sure, tomorrow night, I would not forget my lines even though I'd always forgotten them before. I was thirteen years old now. No matter how nervous I felt standing in front of the whole community, I should be old enough not to mess up my recitation this year.

The only trouble was that the older you were, the longer the piece you were given. This year my recitation was *Et barn er født i Bethlehem*, a Christmas hymn that I was to say as though it were a poem. It had ten verses of only two short lines each, with the refrain *Halleluja, Halleluja* between each verse. Only twenty little lines to learn, and such an easy refrain! Surely I should be able to do that. But it was hard to keep all those tiny verses and their lines from getting mixed up.

I'd practised until I could say those verses in my sleep. Mama had listened patiently as I recited my piece over and over again, coaching me with funny little ways to remember which lines came next.

My second resolution? That I wouldn't eat my apple right away. Every adult and child would be given an apple at the Christmas concert, the only apple all year for most people in our community. This year I planned to save my apple for at least a few minutes—or maybe an hour, or maybe even for a day or so—to enjoy the anticipation of that delicious juicy flavour. Just thinking about it now made the four-mile trip to Dickson a pure pleasure.

The bell in the church tower was already ringing. We hurried to tie our horses to the hitching rail, then said, "Merry Christmas" to everyone on our way into the church.

Golden morning sunshine filled the building. The splendid tree stood at the front of the church. Of course its candles were never lit until the concert on December twenty-sixth.

At the Christmas Day service the congregation sang the old

Danish carols with great gusto—even those of us who couldn't carry a tune if we'd had a bucket.

Listening to the service, one would have thought this was Denmark, not Canada. Our church services were always in Danish. Christmas Day would be no exception. At that age, I assumed God spoke Danish. Everybody's Bibles—and all of Jesus' words in them—were in Danish. We were expected to speak English in our regular school classes. But in home devotions, church services, Sunday school and confirmation classes—anything to do with God—the only acceptable language was Danish.

God was known to us as *Gud* (the "d" is silent). The only time I had ever heard the name of God in English was when a few of the young Danish immigrant men were swearing. Those men hardly ever came to church, but they were at the Christmas service today, dressed in their finest.

After church we went home and had an afternoon nap, then rode in our bobsled to have '' with the neighbours.

At last came the long-awaited night of the Christmas concert. Everyone—dressed in his or her very best—crammed into the church. For that night alone, we Sunday school children had the privilege of sitting in pews set on both sides of the Christmas tree, facing the congregation.

Now the candles on the tree were lit, their flames dancing and sparkling in our excited eyes.

Children, both younger and older than I, took their turns in the Christmas program. They recited hymns, Old Testament prophecies and parts of the Christmas story, while their anxious parents mouthed the well-rehearsed lines. Each time someone forgot words or mixed up their lines, I clenched my jaw, more determined than ever that it wouldn't happen to me this year.

Some children barely managed a nervous whisper; other children shouted. Some mumbled, a few whimpered, others raced through their lines. When it came to their turns, Esther and Thora didn't do too badly at all.

When it came time for me to give my recitation, I stood up, feeling wobbly. I cleared my throat and gulped. I got through both lines of the first verse just fine, then said the refrain, *"Halleluja, Halleluja."*

Now, onward to the second verse. *"Han lagdes i et krybber- rum—."* Oh no, that was the third verse. It had happened again. My face reddened. Papa scowled. But Mama smiled gently, nodding as I stumbled through the rest of the verses, forgot a word here and there, and mixed up a couple more lines.

"For fresler bold og broder blid," I said carefully. Yes, for sure that was the last line of the last verse. I sighed. Then I put my whole heart into the final refrain, *"Halleluja, Halleluja,"* and sat down. After my piece, some older kids forgot their lines too. That helped me feel better.

As always, a few characters—potential auctioneers or preachers—gave perfect performances. My ten-year-old brother Arnfeld was one of those. He had plenty of practice performing at home, where one of our most common games was playing "church". Esther, Thora and I would sit for ages while our brother would stand in front of us as the pastor, holding the T. Eaton catalogue and preaching grand sermons. No wonder Arnfeld could glide through his concert presentation in front of a real congregation!

I decided that I didn't mind too much being one of the nervous line-forgetters. It wasn't so bad when you were used to it. Most people smiled no matter how you performed, and no one would ever dare make fun of you afterwards.

It was time for the special music. How we all loved Fred Pedersen's violin solo! How we looked forward to the choir,

which Fred Pedersen directed, smiling and swinging his whole body to the music.

Neither the children who recited, nor Fred Pedersen's choir, nor any of the other performers, could ever count on finishing their selection in peace.

Rags, buckets of water, and long-handled mops were kept nearby because some of the paper decorations on the tree inevitably caught fire from the candles clipped to the branches. Every year at the concert, people gasped as tall men grabbed wet rags and mops to put out flares. Some of the men would actually crush a small flame with their bare hands.

Tonight, during the recitations, we'd already had two small blazes. First, a paper flower near the very top of the tree had flared. A tall man reached up with his damp mop, and the flame sizzled out immediately. The second was a little paper basket that caught fire. That was touched out with a wet rag.

The third blaze that night was the biggest I had ever seen. It happened during Fred Petersen's violin solo. Fred stopped playing and moved out of the way. The young men who had been standing guard attacked the fire.

This time it wasn't just the paper decorations. "The branches are on fire," someone shouted. Little children cried. Some folks screamed.

Older people called out directions. "Use a coat—"

"Yes, suffocate it," shouted another.

"No. Throw water from the bucket," yelled someone else.

A member of the fire brigade yanked off his heavy jacket, slopped it into the water pail, and laid the soggy thing over the whole burning area of the tree. That did the trick. We all cheered.

Fred Pedersen walked to the front of the church again and continued his sublime violin solo.

There was only one more flare-up that evening—a very minor one—put out immediately by the touch of a damp rag.

During the closing hymn, we children wiggled with excitement, mouths watering, eyes fixed on the candy-filled woven paper baskets hanging from the tree. One of these heart-shaped baskets would be given to each child. I wondered which one I'd get. No two of the baskets, nor the selection of candies therein, were quite alike.

The program was over. The candles on the tree were blown out and the gas lamps were turned up. I stood, holding the blue and white woven paper basket I'd been given, happily trying to decide which candy to eat first. My basket had water stains on it and the candies were a bit damp, but that just made things more interesting.

Then came the best treat. Each person—from toddler to grandparent—was handed a brown paper bag containing some candy, a few peanuts and...the apple!

Most of the children and many of the adults gave in right away. That's what I'd always done too, biting immediately into my apple, juice running down my chin. Much too soon the pleasure would be over. This year was going to be different. I'd still have my apple to enjoy when everyone else's was gone.

I watched and listened and smelled as most of the people crunched into their apples. I held mine, admiring its glossy surface.

Before I realized it, my hand had lifted the apple to my mouth. To my surprise, my teeth were biting into the apple's sweet firmness, and juice was running down my chin.

What a flavour! Maybe next year I'd wait.

Our family rarely went out at night, so even the four-mile ride home in the grain box seemed magical. To the music of the bobsled's metal runners squeaking over frozen snow, and the jingle of the horses' harness, I savoured what remained of my candy. Then I shoved my hands back into my green woollen mitts and watched the stars—God's candles, I called them—sparkling more radiantly than any candles on a tree.

RICHES THIS CHRISTMAS

1 9 2 4

IT WAS LATE NOVEMBER. JUST FOUR MORE WEEKS UNTIL CHRISTMAS. Too bad there was a problem at school.

Every September students were expected to bring money to cover the cost of their school books. This year our parents were having trouble finding enough money for our books. The payment was almost two months overdue. When Arnfeld was milking cows with me one evening, he said, "Archie, you know that Papa and Mama might never get enough cash to pay for our school books. I feel awful whenever the teacher asks us about the money."

"Uh, huh," I said, wanting to return to more pleasant thoughts.

"Well, I'm going to do something about it," said Arnfeld.

"Yeah? What can you do?" I asked, bemused. My brother was only eleven.

"Well," said Arnfeld, "I know that at least one badger has moved onto our land. Way out in the south field. This afternoon I saw three big holes and fresh tracks in the snow all around the holes. I'm going to borrow a trap and set it. We could sell the pelt. Maybe we'd get enough money for some Christmas presents too. Will you help me?"

"Arnfeld, you know badgers are big and strong and mean.

People say that when you've caught a badger in a trap, the badger can attack you and bite your leg right off."

"Archie, we have to get money for school books. Can you think of any other way?"

I couldn't, so I agreed to help. Mama and Papa certainly didn't object when they heard Arnfeld's idea, not only because of the prospect of money for school books, but also because the horses or cows could break a leg in a badger hole.

We borrowed a trap from Trapper Bensen, and set it just within the mouth of what looked like the most used of the big, oval badger holes. Naturally, it was just then that the weather turned so cold, the badger stayed deep within the ground. Day after day there were no fresh tracks to be seen.

Arnfeld kept hoping and praying that somehow he would trap that badger. He checked the trap so often that we teased him, saying he might just as well set up camp there.

The big kids at school had told Arnfeld that, when a badger closed its teeth around a gopher, a mouse, or even a person's ankle, the badger would never release its jaws until it heard bone crushing. If you stuffed egg shells inside your socks or boots (around your ankles), a badger would bite on the egg shells. When it heard the crunching sound of the breaking shells, the badger would say to itself, "I've done my damage," and would let go. But Arnfeld didn't quite believe that story.

Eggshell-free, my little brother kept checking the trap. On a Friday morning, a chinook blew in. The warm wind softened the snow so it was slushy when we walked out to the trap after school. Still no fresh tracks. But the next morning, an excited Arnfeld ran in from the field.

"Archie, come help me. Quick. I can see there's something in the trap."

I grabbed the gun and a long wooden pole before we raced through the snow into the field. The badger was already dead. We wrinkled our noses at its thick, almost skunk-like smell.

We set the trap again in case there was a second badger. The next morning we ran back out to the field. There was a badger in the trap, thrashing about and snarling.

We hit the poor creature over the head, feeling awful. When it lay dead, Arnfeld moaned, "Never again. We're never going to kill another one."

"No," I said, feeling sick to my stomach. "It doesn't matter how much money we could make."

Arnfeld got Trapper Bensen to sell the two badger hides. They brought $6.75 each, enough to pay for all our school books and still leave money for Christmas gifts. We were rich.

But we still felt badly about the badgers.

***

Whenever our neighbour Mr. Lorenzen needed his hair cut and his beard trimmed, he'd come to our place to get Papa to do the job. That year, Mr. Lorenzen arrived about ten days before Christmas so Papa could make him look nice for all the festivities. When the job was finished, Mr. Lorenzen, as always, reached his hand down to hide a twenty-five-cent coin in the hair clippings on the floor. That was for whoever did the sweeping. Esther was waiting with the broom. When she "found" the coin, she handed it to him and said, as was our tradition, "Mr. Lorenzen, this must be yours."

As always, when a sweeper found the coin in the hair cuttings, Mr. Lorenzen smiled and said, "No, it must be yours."

Riches for Esther too!

After Mr. Lorenzen left, we found an envelope on the table. Mr. Lorenzen had written on it, "For Christmas Decorations." Inside was five dollars! Of course we didn't need any Christmas decorations. Mr. Lorenzen knew that our tree was always so laden with beautiful handmade decorations, you could hardly see the branches. We all knew the money was for Christmas presents. More riches!

That afternoon Mama sat down to make out a T. Eaton catalogue order for presents, using the money from Mr. Lorenzen plus what she could spare of her chicken earnings for the year. "Here," said my seven-year-old sister, proudly handing over her coin from the sweepings. "Put my money in too."

Arnfeld had already paid off our school book debt, so he handed the remains of his badger money to Mama. But he had kept back some of the money to buy a present for Mama at Carl Christiansen's general store.

The next morning Papa drove the team and wagon to Dickson to mail Mama's catalogue order. Arnfeld and I came along to shop for Mama's present at the store. Arnfeld found what he wanted right away. "There it is," he said. "Perfect. That brooch. It will look perfect on Mama's good dress." Mama had only one 'good' dress. She had sewn it herself. It was navy and quite plain, but she wore it every Sunday and for any special occasions. The brooch, covered with clear sparkling rhinestones, would indeed be perfect.

Just when I was thinking this Christmas couldn't possibly be any richer, a group of the men in the congregation came up to me after church the next Sunday to ask if I'd like to be one of the fire guards at the concert.

"But I'm only fourteen," I stammered. I was totally unprepared for their request. It was such an honour. Only tall, brave, responsible young men were chosen to stand by with wet rags and mops, to watch for flames on the Christmas tree.

"Look how you've grown, Archie," said one of the men. "You're already taller than most of the congregation. And we think you're quite a young man already. We know you can be depended on to do your best."

I nodded, barely able to speak. My head was swimming with excitement. With no electricity in our community, the lights for a Christmas tree had to be real candles burning brightly amidst handmade paper decorations and resinous spruce branches. Burning candles meant that fires would flare. The tree was always huge, much higher than any person. That's why tall men would be chosen. Fire guards had to be brave too.

Now I really had something to take my mind off the poor dead badgers. Maybe I could help put out a grand Christmas tree fire!

With my thoughts swirling in anticipation of extra-rich Christmas presents and exciting fire duties, Christmas seemed to come so fast.

Our bachelor friends, Mr. Lorenzen and Sam Finnsen, arrived to share our festive Christmas Eve supper of roast chicken, potatoes, peas, sweet-and-sour red cabbage, and carrots. Dessert was scrumptious Danish *Aeble Kage*, made with store-bought dried apples—soaked, then cooked with sugar—layered with sugary sautéed bread crumbs, topped with whipped cream.

After supper Papa took out our old, worn Danish Bible, read the Christmas story, then thanked God for our many blessings. I couldn't help but think of the blessings we'd gotten from the two dead badgers and hoped we'd be forgiven for taking their lives. In his prayer, Papa thanked God for sending His son as a baby to give His life for us.

We all joined hands to sing carols, as we marched around the Christmas tree with the real candles flickering. This would be my practice for the big Christmas tree at the church. I had a pail of water and some rags ready, but only a couple of tiny flares on our tree required attention that evening.

Mama distributed the gifts. Arnfeld and I each received a fascinating board game. There were fine factory-made socks—much softer and less itchy than hand-knit—for Papa, Arnfeld, and me. Esther and even four-year-old Thora each received an elegant necklace made of sparkling glass beads—in pinks and blues. Two-year old Alice got a beautiful little doll. Our new baby brother Walter received a small, stuffed bear. Mr. Lorenzen and Sam Finnsen were delighted with the fancy cookies Mama had made especially for them.

When Mama opened her present, she proudly pinned it on her navy dress. Her eyes—and also Arnfeld's—shone as brightly as the rhinestones of that beautiful brooch.

We played with our new games, then went to bed. Only two more nights until the Christmas concert and my fire duties!

We woke early the next morning to do chores. Then we hitched the horses to the sleigh and drove to Dickson for the Christmas Day church service. Only one more night until the concert. We kids all had parts to learn. I said mine over and over again because I didn't want to forget my recitation amidst the excitement of watching for fires on the tree.

The weather turned very cold that night. The next morning, the thermometer outside the house said thirty-eight below zero Fahrenheit. It was so cold our eyelashes keep freezing shut while we worked outside, feeding the animals, getting water, carrying in wood. It hurt to breathe, even through a scarf. My scarf became coated with white, furry crystals—soggy right where my mouth was and frozen stiff all around.

My head stabbed with pain from the cold. The snow crunched and squeaked as we walked. The sky was bright blue, cloudless. Everything seemed quieter than normal; not a breath of wind disturbed the stillness. When we finished chores, we decided to leave our five milk cows in the crowded barn with the two big chore horses. The other cattle and horses stood out in the cold, heads down, stomping their feet, running around every few minutes to warm up. The hens were in a double-walled, lumber chicken house; but with no light and at such a low temperature, none of them laid eggs.

Two-year-old Alice had a bad cold. She was sneezing and coughing. That afternoon Papa said, "Alice certainly can't go tonight. And Mama, it's much too cold for you and the baby to take the long trip. In fact, it's too cold for Esther and Thora to go too."

Esther and Thora began to cry. Like all of us, they loved the Christmas concert. Besides, they'd miss out on the little brown paper bags and the only fresh apple we'd get all year. Furthermore, they absolutely had to go to the Christmas concert to show off their fabulous new necklaces. How could they stay home and miss out on anything to do with the concert?

Then Papa dropped the bombshell. "And, Archie, you'll have to stay home too. With the weather this cold, Mama will need you here to help her get in wood, keep the fire going, and look after the children and animals. I'll take only one horse and the cutter. Arnfeld can come with me."

"Papa...," I gulped, trying to speak as calmly as possible to avoid angering my father. "I have to go. To help watch the Christmas tree for fires. I promised."

"Archie, if anything goes wrong with the animals here tonight—or with Mama or any of the little kids—we need you to be here."

"But, Papa...," I said.

My father wasn't giving in. "You have to stay home. You're the only one old enough to be any help if anything goes wrong."

There was no point in arguing. Esther and Thora were still sobbing. I was choking back tears myself.

Mama said, "We could still have a Christmas concert. At home. Esther, Thora, Archie—you can say your pieces and we can sing. We'll light the candles on our tree. And Archie, you can watch for fires on it."

And that's just what we did. We waved our sad goodbyes to

Papa and Arnfeld, I finished the outside chores, then we got dressed in our good clothes. Esther and Thora put on their new necklaces; Mama pinned on her brooch. After lighting the candles on the tree, Mama blew out our coal oil lamps. I had my pail of water and rags ready to douse any flames. Together Mama, Esther, Thora, Alice and I sang a few Christmas carols. Mama read devotions and prayed, just like the pastor would be doing at the church Christmas concert.

We each gave the recitations that we'd practised, plus we added in Arnfeld's recitation (which we knew too), and a few others we'd learned from listening at rehearsals. By then I was smiling. It certainly was less nerve-wracking to speak my part in our cozy living room than it would have been to stand in front of the whole congregation. In fact, I didn't forget any of my lines.

Even though our program was a bit disjointed without all of the other recitations, it sounded fine to us. Mama, sitting comfortably on the couch, was our congregation as we each got up to present our memorized piece.

And I was glad that we didn't have any exciting fires on our Christmas tree.

When we finished our recitations, Mama smiled and lifted a finger to her lips. What we heard next was a sound we didn't hear very often—Mama singing all by herself. She sang one of our favourite Christmas carols. We listened in awe. Mama might not have been the best singer in the world; but to us that night, her clear, strong voice filled all the shadows and warmed every corner of our log cabin.

She sang one more Christmas carol alone, another of our very favourites. We sat still, hardly breathing. Even little Thora and Alice, cradled in Mama's arms, were motionless. Then Mama signalled for us to join in the next carol.

And that was the end of our Christmas concert.

We got up then to dance around the tree, singing until we ran out of carols and the candles were burning dangerously low. We blew them out, lit the kerosene lamps and sat without a word, blinking in the bright lamp light.

Mama was almost always too busy to sing to us or even to

visit with us. But that night, after we'd lit the kerosene lamps, she sat on the couch and talked, entertaining us with stories about her life far away and long ago in Denmark. She told us about her mother, who was widowed twice but still married a third time. She related stories about her older half-sister Ane, half-brother Vilhelm and her younger sister Thora, for whom our own sister Thora had been named.

Mama told us about her brother Vilhelm's wife, who was so fussy, she'd send visiting children home if they had a spot on their clothes. And Mama described how, in 1907, she had to get on a huge boat all by herself to travel the thousands of miles from Denmark to Canada. "I was only twenty years old. Just me and my little sewing machine," she said, laughing.

Alice had fallen asleep on the couch. Walter was sleeping soundly in his crib. For a long time we sat, listening to Mama's stories. The only other sounds were the cabin logs creaking loudly from the cold and the soft murmur of the wood, burning and sparking in the cast-iron McClary heater.

It was time for me to go outside to check on the animals and bring in more wood. When I got up to put on my warm clothes, Mama surprised me. "We'll come out with you, Archie—Esther and Thora and I," she said. "Just for a few minutes. To see the stars. They're always extra bright when it's terribly cold. Alice and Walter will be fine sleeping in here alone for a little while."

Excited, Esther and Thora dressed in their warm clothes. Girls and women in those days always wore dresses or skirts, but when it was cold, they pulled two or three pairs of long, thick wool stockings over fleece-lined long underwear so their legs wouldn't freeze. We all had warm, woolen coats that Mama had made (on that same little sewing machine she'd brought with her from Denmark), using the least worn material from men's old coats.

Over our thick wool socks we put our moccasins. We wrapped scarves over our faces, jammed knitted toques down onto our heads, pulled our warmest mitts onto our hands, and headed out into the night. The sharp coldness stabbed our lungs. But the sky was brilliant. No moon, just countless stars splattering the sky. And something else that made us gasp. Soft, green Northern Lights were swinging and swaying like drapes across the north-eastern sky, whispering and swishing.

Among the moving drapes of the Northern Lights we found the North Star, the Big Dipper, then the Little Dipper and Orion's Belt.

"Try to find any place without stars," said Mama. Sure enough, wherever we looked against the velvet black background, more stars would appear.

We stood staring at the sky for what seemed a long time, sucking the icy air through our wool scarves. But it was really only a few minutes before Mama said gently, "Now, let's go with Archie to check on the animals."

We stood in the barn for a time, listening to the one remaining horse and the milk cows peacefully chewing their hay. The barn actually seemed quite warm from the heat of the animals. When we headed back, we walked in silence, our moccasins squeaking in the snow. We filled our arms with wood from the mountainous woodpile, gave one last gaze at the stars and the Northern Lights, then opened the door to our little log house.

Even then, we barely spoke. I stoked the fire in the McClary heater and stuffed in more blocks of wood. We stood huddled around the roaring heater to warm up. Soon Mama began telling more stories—stories of Denmark, when she'd been sixteen and worked on a farm.

It wasn't much longer before we heard a jingling harness, the squeak of the runners, and the horse's hooves crunching through the snow. Before I could get bundled up to go out to help unharness and feed the horse, Papa and Arnfeld flung open the door. They came in, stomping their feet and rubbing their hands. Their eyebrows and the fur of Papa's bearskin coat were white with heavy crystals of frost.

"We had a good Christmas concert here," said Esther, jumping with excitement.

"Our very own Christmas concert," said Thora. "Mama sang. And then—"

"I bet you didn't have any of these," said Papa, reaching into

the big pockets of his bearskin coat and bringing out five little paper bags. "They sent these home just in case somebody might be interested in them." There was one for each of us, including Mama!

After the bountiful presents on Christmas Eve, after our own Christmas concert tonight with Mama's songs and stories, after the Northern Lights and the stars—now here was candy and a whole, juicy apple for each of us. Incredible riches!

Then Papa added, "And, Archie, I have a message for you. Everybody said to tell you that they'll surely be expecting you on fire duty next Christmas."

Muggins the Christmas Dog
1923 AND 1926

FOR YEARS PAPA WORKED AS A CREAM HAULER TO EARN MONEY FOR OUR family.

Dan Morkeberg made butter at his creamery in Markerville, but that was ten miles from Dickson by terrible, rutty trails. It would have been foolish for each farmer to have to haul a gallon or so of cream each week to Markerville. So, once or twice a week, farmers in our area brought their cream as far as Dickson. Papa would drive the four miles from our farm to Dickson, pick up the cream cans, and haul them all to Markerville.

In the summer the farmers would keep their cream cold by hanging the metal cream cans on ropes, down into their hand-dug water wells. The day the cream was to be hauled, the farmers would bring it to Dickson, setting the cans in a water trough to keep them chilled. In the winter, cream cans would simply be left outside the general store, awaiting pickup.

The winter trips were especially hard, at least four or five hours each way. Our team dragged the heavily-loaded bobsled through deep snow, sometimes even fighting a blizzard. Papa left early in the morning and never reached home until suppertime or later.

Mama heated stones in the oven to keep Papa's feet warm under the blankets in the sleigh. Within a few hours the stones cooled, but by then, Papa arrived at Markerville. The people at the creamery would fill an emptied cream can with steaming hot water to keep Papa's feet warm on the trip back home.

One frigid evening, shortly before the Christmas of 1923, I had been out milking the cows. That's why I was the first to greet Papa as he drove the team and bobsled into the yard. "Archie, guess what," said Papa, "I had something different to keep my feet warm on the way home from Markerville tonight."

He lifted the blanket and there, lying on his feet, was a huge puppy with the biggest paws I'd ever seen on a dog.

The pup jumped down from the wagon and romped around me, his tail waving.

"He's ours," said Papa. "From Dan Morkeberg."

I knew that Dan Morkeberg raised Saint Bernard dogs, but why would Papa be bringing one of them to our place? Dan Morkeberg's purebreds were expensive animals, raised for selling to people in towns and cities.

Puzzled, I asked, "A pure Saint Bernard?" The huge, furry pup cavorted about, letting out a series of deep-toned yelps.

"Well, not quite," said Papa. "One of Morkeberg's best Saint Bernards had puppies, but it was obvious this litter wasn't pure-bred. Seems as though the dog had found herself some ordinary neighbourhood boyfriend. Anyway, Morkeberg is giving the puppies away. So I took the biggest one."

The door to the house opened. The rest of the family had heard the yelping. They ran out, as excited as the puppy.

When Mama heard the story, she swooped the pup into her arms and said, "A Christmas present for all of us. Better than games or toys."

Before we went to bed that night, we made a dog house of scrap boards and gave the pup a big dish heaped with warm supper leftovers. He wolfed the food down. Then he looked at us— tail wagging—as if to say, "Is that it?"

Back we went to the house. We filled the pan with bread, dumped in fresh, warm milk, and presented the mixture to the puppy. He gulped that down too.

"The way he eats, this little muggins is going to do some pretty fast growing," said Mama.

"Muggins is a good name," Arnfeld said. We all nodded in agreement.

Muggins loved to eat. Luckily we were on a farm, so there was never a lack of food. Our Christmas pup grew rapidly. It soon became apparent that he was going to take after the

Saint Bernard side of his heritage.

By the time Muggins was a year old, he was gigantic—big enough to look into the windows of the log house while keeping all four feet on the ground. He'd put his big face up to the window, calling us out—his bark rattling the glass.

But Muggins was as gentle as he was large. Muggins would never play rough. We could put our hands in his mouth, and he'd just close his mouth tenderly, his teeth barely touching our skin. Mama could leave our baby brother Walter lying outside on a blanket, and Muggins would stand guard over him.

Muggins never would harm even the smallest baby chick. In fact, he protected our chicks and hens. Until then, the coyotes often sneaked into our yard when we were busy, and murdered a shrieking chicken before we could race to its defence. After we adopted Muggins, we hardly ever lost chickens to the coyotes. Our hens and baby chicks roamed freely, protected by the gentle giant.

"Best Christmas present we ever got," Mama said.

Muggins would chase coyotes from the yard, barking furiously and running into the field after them. If any coyote ever tried to stand up to Muggins, he would pounce, flashing his big teeth, sometimes drawing blood. The coyote would howl and race away. We'd laugh. "I bet that coyote won't be back." Muggins would even take on a whole pack of coyotes if he had to.

But to us children—and to the cats, chickens, and all other little animals—Muggins showed the highest possible degree of gentleness. We all loved him and trusted him implicitly.

Then came the horrible morning one November. Muggins appeared in the yard with a dead turkey in his mouth.

Sick at heart, we took the turkey away from Muggins. Our neighbours, the Lonnebergs, raised turkeys. Any dog that killed a neighbour's fowl would have to be shot immediately. There could be no second chance. Raising fowl was an essential source of food and money for a pioneer family. No one could allow a dog to live if it killed even one chicken or turkey.

A dog that began to kill fowl would always return to kill again. You could hit the dog, even beat him in the face with the dead bird's body, but it wouldn't do any good. Our beloved Muggins would have to be shot. That's all there was to it.

The whole family, including Papa, looked devastated. We'd have to tell the Lonnebergs about their turkey. And it would be better if we could say that we'd already shot the dog.

Papa went into the house to get the gun.

Muggins stood in front of us, blood and feathers stuck to his mouth, wagging his big tail. It was as though he thought he had done something wonderful, as though he was waiting for praise. Mama was silent, holding the dead turkey—looking away.

I couldn't bear to stay around. I knew that Mama and the other kids would go into the house as soon as Papa got the gun and tied Muggins up.

Heart aching, I headed out into the field, feet crunching through the layer of snow that covered the dirt. How I dreaded the sound of that gunshot.

As I walked, I realized that I was following Muggins' huge tracks in the snow—tracks that headed back towards our farm-yard. A spot of blood had dripped here and there beside his tracks. I almost walked away from them, but something kept me following those tracks.

All of a sudden I stopped. There was a terrible mess in the snow. Blood, lots of blood, and turkey feathers. And Muggins' big paw prints. But there were other tracks too. Small paw prints—coyote paw prints. The snow was packed down all around, showing a scuffle...fighting...chunks of bloody fur in the snow.

There were two sets of coyote tracks: one set of tracks coming to the scuffle place from the direction of the Lonneberg farm, the other set heading away from the scuffle place towards the trees. Both sets of coyote tracks were spotted with blood, but the set leading to the trees had much more blood.

Then I realized that a coyote was watching me from the edge of the forest. As I moved towards the animal, it disappeared into the trees. The coyote was limping and bleeding.

I turned and began to run. I ran as fast as I could, yelling, "Stop, Papa, stop! Muggins didn't do it!"

Faster I ran, until my lungs felt as though they would burst. I shouted louder, hoping—praying—that Papa would hear me in time.

Still there was no gunshot.

Papa had heard me before I reached the yard. He stood there waiting, puzzled, the gun in his hand. Muggins, tied short to a tree, was wagging his tail enthusiastically.

The rest of the family had heard my cries. They came out from the house. "He didn't do it," I said, gulping tears. "He was fighting off a coyote. Come and see. Muggins tried to save the turkey. That's why he brought it to us.'

The whole family followed me out into the field. The story was all there in the snow—feathers and blood, with the coyote tracks coming from the direction of the Lonneberg farm.

We stood there, trembling at what had almost happened. Then we realized that we'd left poor Muggins back in the yard, still tied with a rope, tied short to the tree.

In the early spring of 1926, the Lonnebergs moved to British Columbia. We were going to miss our neighbours terribly, but we were thrilled about renting their quarter-section of farmland and their three-bedroom concrete house.

Mr. Soren Peder Lonneberg—usually called SP—was a carpenter, so he had originally built a house of real lumber for his large family. One cold winter night in 1923, their house caught fire.

The flames blazed through the darkness. We could see the

fire from our place half a mile away. Mama, Papa, Arnfeld and I ran and ran through the snow to try to help the Lonnebergs. The rest of it was just like a bad dream of flames and heat and screaming and crying.

In the end, the house was destroyed, but fortunately none of the Lonneberg family was hurt.

SP decided to build his new house using concrete. This proved to be a brilliant idea. Not only was a concrete house more fire-safe, but it also couldn't harbour bedbugs, the curse of pioneers in our area.

By the spring of 1926, there were six children in our family. Mama was expecting another baby in the fall. We'd been feeling a bit crowded—to say the least—in our log house which had only two rooms in total. The two tiny bedrooms in the lean-to barely counted. How unbelievable to think of the Lonnebergs' house with its large living room and kitchen and three real bedrooms. Its floors were shiny linoleum instead of rough planks. And how wonderful to imagine that we wouldn't have to live with bedbugs.

The weather remained very cold when the Lonnebergs left, but we couldn't wait to move. Eagerly we piled our household belongings on the big hay rack, hitched the team to it, and headed for the Lonnebergs' concrete house.

Mama said, "Tomorrow, some of you kids can walk back and bring the two barn cats in your arms. Moving only half a mile away is sure easy, isn't it?"

Whenever we'd left the yard before, we'd always told Muggins to stay home, so he must have been surprised when we called him to follow us and our household possessions. At first he kept trying to turn back, and all the way he lagged a little behind.

When we arrived in the Lonnebergs' yard, Esther said, "Hey, they left their cat." Sure enough, their white cat was strolling towards our wagon. We jumped down, thrilled. We'd always admired that animal's wondrous eyes—one blue, one yellow. Besides, he was so friendly and gentle.

Then the cat saw our enormous Muggins sauntering towards him. The cat hissed, his back arched with his tail straight up. Muggins stopped immediately and flopped quietly onto the ground.

"What happened to the cat's tail?" asked Esther.

I had just noticed it too. There was only a stump left. "It must have frozen off," I said. "A house cat doesn't know that he shouldn't lick himself out in the cold. He isn't used to being outside."

Thora picked up the cat. He purred loudly. But the moment Muggins stood up, the cat hissed. Muggins immediately dropped to the ground again.

"Funny they'd leave their cat without telling us," said Mama, coming up behind us. "But they certainly couldn't have taken him along."

"Yeah," Arnfeld said. "And they knew we loved him. I'm going to call him Soren Peder Lonneberg." Arnfeld laughed. "SP for short. They never called him anything but 'Cat' anyway."

"SP for short," said Thora giggling. "Short, like his tail." The cat was rubbing against her chin.

"Hey," called Papa. "Everybody get over here and help unload all this stuff."

As we carried load after load into the house, Muggins was busy training the cat. SP had to get used to the enormous dog. Muggins worked his way closer and closer.

We were all excited about the cat and the impressive new home, but there was something we realized as we ate supper that night. If we'd been in our log house Muggins could stand, peering in through the windows, watching us, even barking for us to come out to play. This house had a basement that extended above ground, so the windows on the main floor were too high for even Muggins to look into.

There was no way that such a big dog could be inside. But at least he could come into the sheltered veranda and entryway.

Muggins had other things on his mind, though, that evening. By the time we finished supper he could lie just a foot or so away from SP, while the cat watched him in fascination. By the end of the next day, SP knew that he was now part of our family—and therefore under Muggins' protection. But then SP moved into the house to sleep with Thora, so Muggins was left on his own at night again.

In October our little brother Oscar was born—another precious little one for Muggins to protect.

Then came our first Christmas Eve at the concrete house.

Muggins woofed loudly to let us know that our guest had arrived for supper. When we opened the door, our dog was standing beside Mr. Lorenzen in the sheltered entryway. Muggins was wagging his tail, and a purring SP was rubbing against his gigantic legs.

SP sauntered in behind Mr. Lorenzen. We reluctantly closed the door on our big furry friend.

"Mr. Lorenzen," said Alice. "Mama made Thora and me these new dresses. See, they match exactly. And I'm four and Thora's six."

"Oh," said Mr. Lorenzen, smiling. "And you both look so beautiful." The dresses were indeed fancy, made of orange and yellow flowered material, sewn with scalloped cream-coloured collars.

After supper we took out to Muggins his huge dish heaped with warm table scraps. Mama had cut a thick slab of fresh roast pork to lay on top, saying, "Because it's Christmas." With his tail swinging from side to side, Muggins devoured the festive dinner.

As always, after Christmas Eve devotions, we lit the dozens of candles on the tree and danced around it, singing carols. Thora twirled and pranced, proudly swirling the full, round skirt of her new dress.

Suddenly, Mama was hitting Thora, spanking her on the bottom, again and again. "Thora! Thora!" Mama yelled.

Thora howled. Why would Mama hit her? Then we realized that the back of Thora's skirt was on fire from a Christmas tree candle, and Mama was trying to beat out the flames. Papa grabbed the blanket off a bed. He and Mr. Lorenzen wrapped Thora in the blanket, suffocating the fire.

What was left of Thora's dress certainly didn't match Alice's any more. Wailing, Thora changed into an everyday dress.

"If Muggins could have looked in these windows," said Esther, "he would have seen the fire. He would have barked to warn us."

"He probably would have," said Mama, smiling.

As always, when any of us used the outdoor toilet that evening, Muggins followed along through the snow. He'd wait there while people did their business, then follow back to the sheltered entryway until the next person made the trek.

Just before I went to bed, almost midnight, I decided to pay a last visit to the outhouse. There, in the entryway, Muggins lay quietly. Not wanting to wake him, I crept past, and went outside. When I came back, I couldn't resist bending over to give him a good-night pat for Christmas Eve. But the dog didn't wag his tail or move at all when I touched him.

"Muggins," I called. He still didn't move. I pushed him up, but he just flopped back down.

"Help!" I yelled. "Something's wrong with Muggins!" Everyone came running.

Papa listened against Muggins' chest. "No! He's dead. What happened to him?"

I moaned. "He was just lying here."

In shock we all knelt beside Muggins. SP rubbed against him, meowing.

"He must have had a heart attack," said Mr. Lorenzen, shaking his head in disbelief. "Or a twisted bowel or something."

"My Muggins." Mama's voice sounded squeaky and feeble. "My dear Muggins. Who's going to protect us and the chickens?"

"He always protected us," Esther said, wiping at her tears. "When a stranger drove in the yard—"

Arnfeld nodded. "He'd bark so hard. Wouldn't let any stranger near us. Until we said it was OK."

"But, Muggins, you never acted rough with us," Thora said, leaning her face against his thick fur. "Never. No matter how rough we played with you."

We stayed beside the dog, hugging him, stroking him, hardly knowing what to do or say. Alice and Walter clung to Mama. She held them tightly.

Arnfeld broke the silence. "When Muggins tried to rescue the Lonnebergs' turkey from the coyote..." He couldn't finish his sentence. We all looked down, remembering that awful November day.

"We should have known," I said. "Muggins would never have done anything bad."

Papa swallowed hard. Mama cradled the huge, limp head beside her face. Shivering from cold, but reluctant to leave him out there on the porch, we stroked the enormous furry body, our breath like smoke in the frigid air.

"How are we going to get along without him?" Thora said. "He was our friend."

Eventually we had to go into the house. We stood around the heater, shaking, trying to warm up the ice-cold feeling inside of us.

"Strange," said Mama, "Muggins came to us—and now he has left us—at the same time of the year." She sighed, struggling to continue. "We'll always remember him, you know. But especially every Christmas."

MAMA'S CHICKENS AND THE PHOTOS
1 9 3 9

MAMA AND PAPA AND MY YOUNGER SIBLINGS STILL FARMED THE OLD homestead, but they no longer rented the Lonneberg place. Our original pioneer home had become just a heap of rotting logs.

The family had grown. In 1928 Ella was born. Paul—Mama's tenth and last baby—arrived in 1931. That year we had built a new home. It was a good, two-storey house made from lumber that had come from our own woodland trees.

By 1939, I was twenty-nine and could hardly believe how quickly things were changing. The older siblings were away most of the time. My sister Thora was working in Calgary and had just announced her engagement. Esther had a job in Innisfail and was busy making marriage plans too. Arnfeld and I were both in Calgary at college, planning to finish our last years of university and seminary in the United States. Altogether there were nine of us siblings—Irene had died as a baby—who now saw each other only during holidays and the odd weekend.

Mama had remarked that her two eldest sons (Arnfeld and I) showed almost as much interest in two young women as we did in our studies. Mama seemed acutely aware, as I was, of further changes that were impending for us all.

One spring evening when I happened to be home and chatting about future plans, Mama turned to Papa and said, "We should have a professional portrait taken of our family. All eleven of us, while we can still get everybody together."

Papa snorted. "Have you lost your mind? Where would we ever find money for a professional portrait? With this never-ending depression, we're having a hard enough time finding money for sugar and coffee."

"But this is important," Mama said. "Before they all go off in separate directions. It's probably our last chance. This is our family."

"Important!" Papa was almost shouting. "You'd waste grocery and clothing money for something as frivolous as getting a picture taken? It would probably cost more than Thora or Esther earn in a month. Have you gone crazy?"

"But, Papa," I said, "Mama's right. It would be something worth having—"

"Archie, you keep out of this." Papa glared at me.

Mama kept talking. "Papa, if we get a photo taken, we could give each of the kids a copy for their Christmas present. I'd use some of the chicken money, just like I do every Christmas."

"The kids can each have a pair of socks for Christmas," said Papa. "Do you have any idea how much studio photographs cost? We need the money from the chickens just to keep surviving."

"But, Papa—," said Mama.

"Absolutely not," Papa thundered. "There is no money, no extra money, not for anything. Certainly there's no money for a picture. There is no extra money."

Mama set her chin resolutely. "Then this year I'll raise more chickens."

"More chickens just mean more work looking after them, and more chickens for the coyotes to eat."

Mama couldn't argue with this. It didn't matter how carefully she locked her chickens in the coop at night. Farm chickens did have to roam freely to eat during the day, and a dependable chicken-guarding dog was hard to find. We hadn't found another dog to match Muggins. During the past few summers the coyotes had been very hard on Mama's chicken population.

Still, this was one project that my mother was determined to accomplish. "Well, I'll pray that this summer the coyotes decide they prefer rabbit stew to chicken pie."

"Who's going to buy all these extra chickens when you're finished raising them?" Papa asked. "Nobody has any money."

"Well, I'll have to pray about that too."

Somehow my mother's prayers, which followed her brood of children all through their lifetime, must have also followed her brood of chickens throughout that summer and fall. It was her most successful year in the poultry business.

Arnfeld and I worked away from home that summer. But whenever possible we had to come back to the farm to help Papa with field work and harvesting. That meant we had the privilege of witnessing the proceedings with Mama's photo project.

Mama never bought baby chicks—she always raised her own. She had about twenty hens and a rooster. If any hen began to sit on her nest all day rather than roam the yard, she was called "broody." Only a broody hen would remain on the nest to keep the fertilized eggs warm—they took three weeks to hatch.

Usually most hens didn't turn broody. They just laid an egg each morning and spent the rest of the day wandering the yard, eating insects and grass. That year it seemed that a higher-than-usual number of Mama's hens were broody.

Mama had little "brood hen houses," made of scrap boards, in various places around the yard. She put each broody hen in one of these houses and gave her about a dozen eggs to sit on. Usually some of the eggs didn't hatch. But this year, it seemed as though a high proportion of the eggs did hatch. Soon many hens and their flocks of fluffy yellow chicks were out scratching in the yard in the daytime.

At night Mama carefully locked up each hen and her rapidly growing chicks. The rest of Mama's hens, the non-broody ones, kept producing eggs for our family to eat every day.

About the beginning of July, one of Mama's best egg-laying hens had disappeared. We looked all over for the hen, but she was nowhere to be found. We assumed the worst, that a coyote had managed to catch her.

Just over three weeks later, Mama came running into the house, laughing. "I have a whole extra flock of new chicks!" The missing hen, which had not showed any signs of broodiness, must have decided to do things her own way. She had found a hiding place somewhere in the woods, laid her eggs, hatched a family, then paraded her little chicks back into the yard to Mama.

The dozens and dozens of chicks from all those hens soon lost their fluffiness and began to grow normal feathers. They put on weight due to the rich, green grass, abundant summer insects and Mama's grain feedings. Soon the yard was full of healthy, young adult chickens.

That fall my mother worked very hard, butchering, plucking and cleaning chickens. The smell of chicken guts and wet feathers hung heavily around the yard each evening when we came home from harvesting. We thought of all the hungry people those chickens would feed.

The Depression was easing up by then, so Carl Christiansen at our general store had no trouble finding buyers in Calgary for Mama's delicious, tender farm chickens. And the prices were surprisingly high.

Mama set an afternoon date with George's Photo Studio in the town of Innisfail, twenty-five miles away. Even in 1939, that was a considerable distance. Because of the Depression, many farmers—including our family—had abandoned their new-fangled cars and gone back to using teams and wagons. Farm horses required no cash to fuel or maintain. But the road from Dickson to Innisfail was thick, gooey mud or deep, hard ruts—difficult for horse-pulled wagons as well as vehicles.

Still, even Papa would not have dared to argue at this point. Those of us who had jobs or were in college knew that we had better clear that afternoon date on our calendar. Arnfeld and I took the train about eighty miles, from Calgary to Innisfail. The whole family assembled at George's Studio, preened and dressed to look our very best.

The sale of Mama's many chickens gave her enough money to order one large photo and nine small ones. Because the photos were to be gifts from Mama that year, none of us, not even Papa, was allowed to see them. We would have to wait until Christmas Eve.

That year, as always, we had our celebration and festivities on Christmas Eve. But things were a little different now. We all spoke English, even to chat and to tell jokes. That night, as we marched around the Christmas tree, we sang almost all the carols in English. Only one or two of our absolute favourites that had no English equivalent were still belted out in Danish. When Papa read the Christmas story to us that night, instead of picking up his old tattered Danish Bible, he used a new English one. He even prayed in English.

When it came time to hand out the presents, Mama did the honours as always. That evening Mama first handed Papa the biggest package from under the Christmas tree. As Papa took off the wrapping paper, we all gathered around, holding our breath. We gasped as we saw the photo. It was beautifully framed. And how wonderful we all looked. This family picture was a treasure to be passed on for generations, just as Mama had known.

Mama reached under the Christmas tree to hand her gift to each of her nine children. We tore the wrapping paper off to see our very own copy of the family photograph, each one mounted in a fancy, grey studio presentation folder.

I held my photo close, grateful that Mama's chickens had bought a gift that would freeze this moment and give us something to hold onto, even when everything kept changing. No other Christmas present could have had as much meaning.

Some of us would be leaving again, too soon, to go back to work or school. Next year I'd be thousands of miles away, in the eastern United States. Our family would not be together at Christmas for at least two or three more years. But we would have this photo to accompany us throughout our lives, wherever we settled.

Mama took the large, framed photograph and set it in the place of honour on top of our old organ. Later that evening I noticed Mama standing there, admiring the impressive picture of her family—gazing at it with pure joy.

"Hey, Mama," I asked, grinning, "which are you the most proud of? Your family? Or your chickens?"

Mama laughed. And I was elated to see that Papa's eyes were on Mama, his face lit with a wide smile.

PEBBERNODDERS

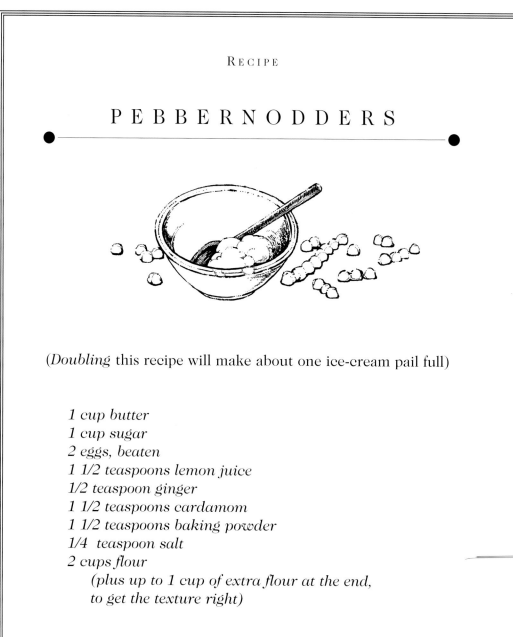

(*Doubling* this recipe will make about one ice-cream pail full)

    1 cup butter
    1 cup sugar
    2 eggs, beaten
    1 1/2 teaspoons lemon juice
    1/2 teaspoon ginger
    1 1/2 teaspoons cardamom
    1 1/2 teaspoons baking powder
    1/4 teaspoon salt
    2 cups flour
        (plus up to 1 cup of extra flour at the end,
        to get the texture right)

- Leave the butter at room temperature for at least a few hours or overnight to soften it. (Don't try to soften the butter in the microwave. It might melt, and wreck the pebbernodders).

- Set the oven to 350° F.

- With a beater, mix the soft butter with the sugar, beaten eggs, and lemon juice.

- Mix all dry ingredients (flour, ginger, cardamom, salt and baking powder). Sift the dry ingredient mixture into the softened butter mixture. Mix well with a big spoon, then work the dough with your hands into a ball. It will be very soft at this point. Place the ball of dough on the counter.

- Put the 1 cup of extra flour into a sifter or a cup. Mix some of this extra flour into the cookie dough, testing with each small addition. You will probably need about half of this cup of flour, but you never know exactly how much from one time to the next. You have added just the right amount of flour when the dough doesn't stick to your hands, and when it rolls into nice snakes without coming apart.

- Roll the dough on the counter, about a handful at a time, using your fingers or palms to make narrow snakes. Chop across the snakes to make tiny cookies about the size of a fingertip. Put the cookies (not touching each other) on ungreased cookie sheets.

- Bake 3 minutes on the lower oven rack, then about 4 to 8 minutes on the higher rack until the pebbernodders are light brown. Or you can bake them the whole time on the middle rack of your oven. Watch them carefully—they burn easily.

- With a spatula, scrape the cookies off the pans onto sheets of brown paper (paper bags cut open are fine) to cool. The pebbernodders should be completely cooled before storing.

Make Your Own Angel Ladders

Archie's parents learned to make angel ladders
in Denmark more than a hundred years ago.

1. Take a single sheet of tissue paper. With your scissors, cut a long strip about two inches wide. Actually, angel ladders can be any size you want, but the tissue strips should be the same width from top to bottom.

2. Fold the strip in half lengthwise. The strip will be about one inch wide now.

3. Fold the strip again, but this time from top to bottom.

4. Repeat step 3 a few more times until you have a length of only about three inches and several layers thick. One side of the strip will be open edges, the other side will be folded edges.

5. With your scissors, cut a whole row of slits through the layers of the folded edge. Make your slits around 3/4-inch long and 1/4-inch apart. These slits will form the rungs of your ladder, so you'll want to cut each slit the same length. Be sure to cut a slit in the doubled-up ends too, so your ladder won't be missing any rungs.

6. Unfold the paper carefully so the slits don't tear. Stretch out the ladder gently to separate the rungs from each other.

Hang the top rung of your angel ladder on a Christmas tree branch. You can anchor the bottom rung of your angel ladder to a branch below, or leave the lower end free. Either way, the tissue paper will move and sway with the air currents as though invisible little angels are climbing your ladder.

Now that you've made your first angel ladder, you can experiment with the next ones. If you want a space between your rungs, simply snip away every second rung (at the folded stage). Try cutting various sizes of angel ladders. See how tiny and precise you can make them.

About the Author

Irene Morck was born in St. John, New Brunswick. She has lived in Manitoba, Saskatchewan, Alberta, and the Caribbean. Irene received a B.Sc. (Honours in Biochemistry) from the University of Alberta and a teaching certificate from the University of Calgary. She taught science at boys' schools in Barbados, and in Kingston, Jamaica. While in Jamaica, she also did two years of biochemistry research at the University of the West Indies.

Irene is the author of *A Question of Courage, Between Brothers, Tough Trails, Tiger's New Cowboy Boots* and *Five Pennies: A Prairie Boy's Story.*

Irene and her husband Mogens Nielsen live on a farm in central Alberta, only a few kilometres from Dickson. They enjoy freelance photography, riding their mules, travelling, learning Spanish, and hiking.

About the Illustrator

Muriel Wood was born in Kent, England. She obtained her diploma in design and painting at the Canterbury College Art of before immigrating to Canada. Since the early 1960's, Muriel's work has appeared in many places: magazines, books, stamps, porcelains, posters and on canvas in group and one-woman shows. Muriel's children's books include L.M. Montgomery's *Anne of Green Gables* and both celebrated editions of Margaret Laurence's *The Olden Days Coat,* which earned her a permanent place in the Museum of Illustration at the Society of Illustrators in New York.

Muriel is an instructor at the Ontario College of Art and Design in Toronto, Ontario. She lives in a Victorian house overlooking the park in Toronto's historic Cabbagetown with her husband David Chestnut and two cats.

ACKNOWLEDGEMENTS

Special thanks to the Toronto Public Library Picture Reference Department.

M.W.

Thank you to Gail Winskill for the creativity and dreams that led to this book. Thanks to Ann Featherstone, who patiently (and with good humour) helped me make the stories so much better. Thanks to Muriel Wood for her artistic talent plus her painstaking attention to detail. Thank you to Mogens, my husband and my friend, for always being there when I needed him.

I.M.